COAHUILACERATOPS

DIAMANTINASAURUS

QIANZHOUSAURUS

CAIUAJARA

YUTYRANNUS

PRESTOSUCHUS

BALAUR

AMPELO

CHEIRUS

JANE YOLEN

How Do Dinosaurs Choose Their PETS?

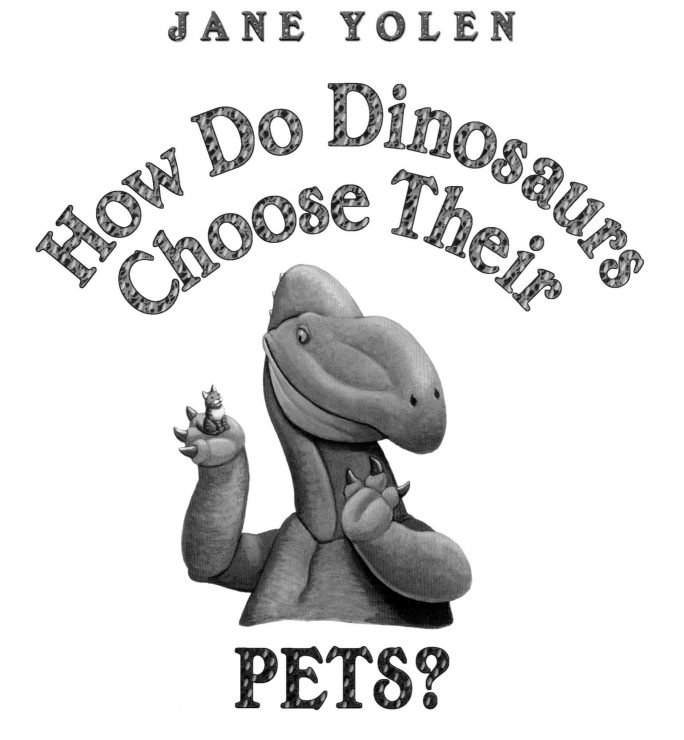

Illustrated by
MARK TEAGUE

THE BLUE SKY PRESS
An Imprint of Scholastic Inc. · New York

THE BLUE SKY PRESS

Library of Congress catalog card number: 2015046567

ISBN 978-1-338-03278-9

10 9 8 7 6 5 4 3 2 1   17 18 19 20 21

Printed in Malaysia   108
First edition, January 2017

Book design by Kathleen Westray

A special book for Sam—J. Y.

For Laura—M. T.

Ow does a dinosaur

pick out his pet?

Does he go on the prowl

with a stick and a net?

Does he head to the zoo
and take home a big cat?
(And what does his mom
have to say about that?)

Does she drag a huge elephant
back in a wagon
with both its long trunk
and its wee tail

a-dragging?

Or, speaking of dragons,

does she go acquire

a high-flying beastie

who loves to

breathe fire?

Does he pick out
a boa constrictor for play?
Does it look at his dog
in a very odd way?

AMPELOSAURUS

Does he sneak an iguana

inside of a cap?

Or lead home a kangaroo

by a long strap?

Does he ask for a manatee,

maybe a whale,

or wish for a shark

he can keep in a pail?

Does she carry off tortoises,

zebras, a mink?

Giving them hay

and a cola to drink?

Is that what you think?

No . . . a dinosaur doesn't.
She knows what to do,
and she never brings anything
home from the zoo.

DO NOT FEED

He goes to a shelter

or pet store

or farm

to find a small creature

who will do no harm.

He brings home a kitten
or hamster or pup
that he can teach manners
as they both grow up.

She cares for her pet,
and gives love

even more.

Big hugs to your friend,

little dinosaur.

COAHUILACERATOPS

DIAMANTINASAURUS

QIANZHOUSAURUS

CAIUAJARA

PRESTOSUCHUS

YUTYRANNUS

RHINOREX

BALAUR

AMPELOSAURUS

DEINOCHEIRUS